For Lena, with love

First published 2021 by Walker Books Ltd,
87 Vauxhall Walk, London, SE11 5HJ

2 4 6 8 10 9 7 5 3

Illustrations © 1988–2021 Shirley Hughes
Introduction © 2021 Shirley Hughes

This book has been typeset in Plantin

Printed in China

British Library Cataloguing in Publication Data:
a catalogue record for this book is available
from the British Library

ISBN: 978-1-4063-9031-5

www.walker.co.uk

ROUND AND ROUND THE GARDEN

A FIRST BOOK OF NURSERY RHYMES

Shirley Hughes

WALKER BOOKS
AND SUBSIDIARIES
LONDON · BOSTON · SYDNEY · AUCKLAND

CONTENTS

Playtime Rhymes

Animal Rhymes

Action Rhymes

Bedtime Rhymes

A NOTE FROM SHIRLEY HUGHES

This classic collection has some of my favourite nursery rhymes from childhood, and some new ones too! You and your toddler can sing and play along to these rhymes all through the day, whether you are walking to nursery on a cold and frosty morning, splashing about in a tub or going to bed. I hope that my illustrations capture the fun to be had and inspire a new generation to discover their favourite nursery rhymes.

Shirley Hughes

PLAYTIME RHYMES

Girls and boys come out to play

Girls and boys come out to play,
The moon doth shine as bright as day;
Leave your supper, and leave your sleep,
And come with your playfellows into the street.

Come with a whoop, come with a call,
Come with a good will or not at all.
Up the ladder and down the wall,
A halfpenny roll will serve us all.

Swing high

Swing high, swing high,
Away we go.
Up to the trees
Where the breezes blow,
Where the birdies nest
And play all day,
And all the world
Is bright and gay.

How many days

How many days has my baby to play?
Saturday, Sunday, Monday,
Tuesday, Wednesday, Thursday, Friday,
Saturday, Sunday, Monday.

Ride a cock-horse to Banbury Cross

Ride a cock-horse to Banbury Cross,
To see a fine lady upon a white horse;
Rings on her fingers and bells on her toes,
And she shall have music wherever she goes.

Rub-a-dub-dub

Rub-a-dub-dub,
Three men in a tub,
And who do you think they be?
The butcher, the baker, the candlestick maker,
And all of them gone to sea.

Whether the weather be fine

Whether the weather be fine,
Or whether the weather be not,
Whether the weather be cold,
Or whether the weather be hot,
We'll weather the weather
Whatever the weather,
Whether we like it or not!

I hear thunder

~

I hear thunder, I hear thunder,
Hark don't you, hark don't you?
Pitter patter raindrops, pitter patter raindrops,
I'm wet through, so are you!

Doctor Foster went to Glo'ster

~

Doctor Foster went to Glo'ster in a shower of rain.
He stepped in a puddle, right up to his middle,
And never went there again.

Rain, rain, go away

Rain, rain, go away,
Come again another day.
Rain, rain, go away,
Little Katie wants to play.

I'm the king of the castle

I'm the king of the castle,
Get down you dirty rascal!

One, two, buckle my shoe

One, two, buckle my shoe!
Three, four, knock at the door!
Five, six, pick up sticks;
Seven, eight, lay them straight;
Nine, ten, a big fat hen!

Cobbler, cobbler

Cobbler, cobbler, mend my shoe,
Get it done by half-past two.
Half-past two is far too late!
Get it done by half-past eight.

There was an old woman who lived in a shoe

There was an old woman
Who lived in a shoe.
She had so many children
She didn't know what to do.
She gave them some honey
With butter and bread;
And kissed them all soundly
And put them to bed.

Jack and Jill

Jack and Jill went up the hill
To fetch a pail of water.
Jack fell down and broke his crown,
And Jill came tumbling after.
Up Jack got, and home did trot,
As fast as he could caper,
He went to bed to mend his head,
With vinegar and brown paper.

Polly put the kettle on

Polly put the kettle on,
Polly put the kettle on,
Polly put the kettle on,
We'll all have tea.

If all the world was apple pie

If all the world was apple pie,
And all the sea was ink,
And all the trees were bread and cheese,
What should we have for drink?

The man in the moon

The man in the moon,
Came tumbling down,
And asked his way to Norwich,
He went by the south,
And burnt his mouth
With supping cold pease-porridge.

Five currant buns

Five currant buns in a baker's shop,
Big and round with a cherry on the top.
Along came a boy with a penny one day,
Bought a currant bun and took it away.

Hot-cross buns

Hot-cross buns! Hot-cross buns!
One a penny, two a penny,
Hot-cross buns!
If you have no daughters,
Give them to your sons.
One a penny, two a penny,
Hot-cross buns!

To market, to market

To market, to market,
To buy a plum bun.
Home again, home again,
Market is done.

This little piggy went to market

This little piggy went to market,
This little piggy stayed at home,
This little piggy had roast beef,
This little piggy had none.
And this little piggy went...
"Wee, wee, wee," all the way home.

The Queen of Hearts

The Queen of Hearts,
She made some tarts,
All on a summer's day;
The Knave of Hearts,
He stole those tarts,
And took them clean away.
The Queen of Hearts
Called for the tarts,
And beat the knave full sore;
The Knave of Hearts
Brought back the tarts,
And vowed he'd steal no more.

Little Miss Muffet

Little Miss Muffet
Sat on a tuffet,
Eating her curds and whey;
Along came a spider,
Who sat down beside her,
And frightened Miss Muffet away.

Mary, Mary, quite contrary

Mary, Mary, quite contrary,
How does your garden grow?
With silver bells and cockle-shells,
And pretty maids all in a row.

London Bridge is falling down

London Bridge is falling down,
Falling down, falling down.
London Bridge is falling down,
My fair lady.

ANIMAL RHYMES

Three little kittens

Three little kittens, they lost their mittens,
And they began to cry,
"Oh, mother dear, we sadly fear,
That we have lost our mittens."
"What! Lost your mittens, you naughty kittens!
Then you shall have no pie."
"Meow, meow, meow."
"Then you shall have no pie."

Three little kittens, they found their mittens,
And they began to cry,
"Oh, mother dear, see here, see here,
For we have found our mittens."
"Put on your mittens, you silly kittens,
And you shall have some pie."
"Purr, purr, purr,
Oh, let us have some pie."

Pusssycat, pussycat

"Pussycat, pussycat, where have you been?"
"I've been up to London to visit the Queen."
"Pussycat, pussycat, what did you do there?"
"I frightened a little mouse under her chair.
MEOW!"

Five little ducks

Five little ducks went swimming one day,
Over the hill and far away.
Mother duck said, "Quack, quack, quack, quack!"
And only four little ducks came back.

Four little ducks went swimming one day,
Over the hill and far away.
Mother duck said, "Quack, quack, quack, quack!"
And only three little ducks came back.

Three little ducks went swimming one day,
Over the hill and far away.
Mother duck said, "Quack, quack, quack, quack!"
And only two little ducks came back.

Two little ducks went swimming one day,
Over the hill and far away.
Mother duck said, "Quack, quack, quack, quack!"
And only one little duck came back.

One little duck went swimming one day,
Over the hill and far away.
Mother duck said, "Quack, quack, quack, quack!"
And all her five little ducks came back.

There's a worm at the bottom of the garden

There's a worm at the bottom of the garden,
And his name is Wiggly Woo.
There's a worm at the bottom of the garden,
And all that he can do
Is wiggle all night
And wiggle all day
Whatever else the people do say.
There's a worm at the bottom of the garden,
And his name is Wiggly Woo.

One, two, three, four, five

One, two, three, four, five,
Once I caught a fish alive,
Six, seven, eight, nine, ten,
Then I let it go again.
Why did you let it go?
Because it bit my finger so.
Which finger did it bite?
This little finger on the right.

Once I saw a little bird

Once I saw a little bird
Come hop, hop, hop;
So I cried, "Little bird,
Will you stop, stop, stop?"
And was going to the window,
To say, "How do you do?"
But he shook his little tail,
And far away he flew.

Two little dicky birds

Two little dicky birds
Sitting on a wall.
One named Peter,
The other named Paul.
Fly away Peter,
Fly away Paul,
Come back Peter,
Come back Paul.

Old MacDonald had a farm

Old MacDonald had a farm,
Ee-eye, ee-eye-oh!
And on that farm he had a duck,
Ee-eye, ee-eye-oh!
With a "quack, quack" here,
And a "quack, quack" there,
Here a "quack," there a "quack,"
Everywhere a "quack, quack!"
Old MacDonald had a farm,
Ee-eye, ee-eye-oh!

Old MacDonald had a farm,
Ee-eye, ee-eye-oh!
And on that farm he had a dog,
Ee-eye, ee-eye-oh!
With a "woof, woof" here,
And a "woof, woof" there,
Here a "woof," there a "woof,"
Everywhere a "woof, woof!"
Old MacDonald had a farm,
Ee-eye, ee-eye-oh!

Old MacDonald had a farm,
Ee-eye, ee-eye-oh!
And on that farm he had a pig,
Ee-eye, ee-eye-oh!
With an "oink, oink" here,
And an "oink, oink" there,
Here an "oink," there an "oink,"
Everywhere an "oink, oink!"
Old MacDonald had a farm,
Ee-eye, ee-eye-oh!

Mary had a little lamb

Mary had a little lamb,
Its fleece was white as snow;
And everywhere that Mary went
The lamb was sure to go.

Little Bo-Peep

Little Bo-Peep has lost her sheep,
And can't tell where to find them;
Leave them alone, and they'll come home,
Wagging their tails behind them.

ACTION RHYMES

Ring-a-ring o' roses

Ring-a-ring o' roses,
A pocket full of posies,
A-tishoo! A-tishoo!
We all fall down!

Round and round the garden

Round and round the garden,
Like a teddy bear.
One step, two step,
Tickle you under there!

Pat-a-cake

Pat-a-cake, pat-a-cake, baker's man.
Make me a cake as fast as you can.
Pat it and prick it and mark it with B,
And put it in the oven for baby and me.

This is the way the ladies ride

This is the way the ladies ride: trit-trot, trit-trot.

This is the way the gentlemen ride: tarran, tarran.

This is the way the farmers ride: clip-clop, clip-clop.

This is the way the jockeys ride: gallopy, gallopy,

And FALL OFF!

Oh, the grand old Duke of York

Oh, the grand old Duke of York,
He had ten thousand men,
He marched them up to the top of the hill
And he marched them down again.
And when they were up, they were up,
And when they were down, they were down,
And when they were only half way up
They were neither up nor down.

Zoom, zoom, zoom

Zoom, zoom, zoom,
We're going to the moon!
Zoom, zoom, zoom,
We'll be there very soon.

If you want to take a trip,
Climb on board my rocket ship.
Zoom, zoom, zoom,
We're going to the moon!
Five-four-three-two-one BLAST OFF!

Row, row, row your boat

Row, row, row your boat,
Gently down the stream,
Merrily, merrily, merrily, merrily,
Life is but a dream.

A sailor went to sea, sea, sea

A sailor went to sea, sea, sea,
To see what he could see, see, see.
But all that he could see, see, see,
Was the bottom of the deep blue sea, sea, sea.

Oranges and lemons

"Oranges and lemons,"
Say the bells of Saint Clement's.
"You owe me five farthings,"
Say the bells of Saint Martin's.
"When will you pay me?"
Say the bells of Old Bailey.
"When I grow rich,"
Say the bells of Shoreditch.
"When will that be?"
Say the bells of Stepney.
"I do not know,"
Say the great bells of Bow.

Peekaboo! Peekaboo!

Peekaboo! Peekaboo!

I see you!

Where is sister?

Peekaboo! Peekaboo!

I see you!

Where is brother?

Peekaboo! Peekaboo!

I see you!

Where is baby?

Peekaboo! Peekaboo!

I see you!

Humpty Dumpty sat on a wall

Humpty Dumpty sat on a wall,
Humpty Dumpty had a great fall;
All the king's horses
And all the king's men
Couldn't put Humpty together again.

Incy Wincy spider

Incy Wincy spider climbed up the water spout,
Down came the rain and washed the spider out,
Out came the sunshine and dried up all the rain,
And Incy Wincy spider climbed up the spout again.

Here we go round the mulberry bush

Here we go round the mulberry bush,
The mulberry bush,
The mulberry bush.
Here we go round the mulberry bush
On a cold and frosty morning.

This is the way we wash our face,
Wash our face,
Wash our face.
This is the way we wash our face
On a cold and frosty morning.

This is the way we comb our hair,
Comb our hair,
Comb our hair.
This is the way we comb our hair
On a cold and frosty morning.

This is the way we brush our teeth,
Brush our teeth,
Brush our teeth.
This is the way we brush our teeth
On a cold and frosty morning.

Five in the bed

There were five in the bed and the little one said,
"Roll over, roll over!"
So they all rolled over and one fell out.

There were four in the bed and the little one said,
"Roll over, roll over!"
So they all rolled over and one fell out.

There were three in the bed and the little one said,
"Roll over, roll over!"
So they all rolled over and one fell out.

There were two in the bed and the little one said,
"Roll over, roll over!"
So they all rolled over and one fell out.

There was one in the bed and the little one said,
"Good night!"

BEDTIME RHYMES

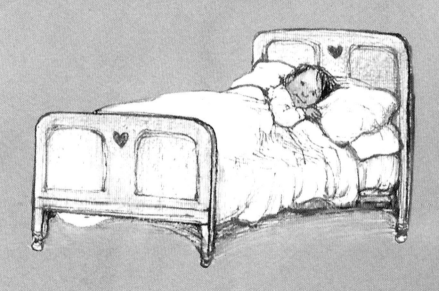

Diddle, diddle dumpling

Diddle, diddle dumpling, my son John,
Went to bed with his trousers on.
One shoe off and the other shoe on,
Diddle, diddle dumpling, my son John.

Come, let's to bed

"Come, let's to bed," says Sleepy-Head.
"Tarry a while," says Slow.
"Put on the pot," says Greedy-Gut.
"Let's sup before we go."

Teddy bear, teddy bear

Teddy bear, teddy bear,
Turn around!
Teddy bear, teddy bear,
Touch the ground!
Teddy bear, teddy bear,
Jump up high!
Teddy bear, teddy bear,
Touch the sky!

Teddy bear, teddy bear,
Bend down low!
Teddy bear, teddy bear,
Touch your toes!
Teddy bear, teddy bear,
Turn out the light!
Teddy bear, teddy bear,
Say good night!

Twinkle, twinkle, little star

Twinkle, twinkle, little star,
How I wonder what you are!
Up above the world so high,
Like a diamond in the sky.
Twinkle, twinkle, little star,
How I wonder what you are!

Star light, star bright

Star light, star bright,
First star I see tonight,
I wish I may, I wish I might,
Have the wish I wish tonight.

Rock-a-bye, baby

Rock-a-bye, baby
On the treetop.
When the wind blows,
The cradle will rock.
When the bough breaks,
The cradle will fall,
And down will come baby,
Cradle and all.

Little Boy Blue

Little Boy Blue, come blow your horn,
The sheep's in the meadow, the cow's in the corn.
Where is that boy who looks after the sheep?
He's under a haystack, fast asleep.

Sleep, baby, sleep

Sleep, baby, sleep,
Thy father tends the sheep.
Thy mother shakes the dreamland tree
To shake dreams down on thee.
Sleep, baby, sleep,
Sleep, baby, sleep.